DEATH GRIP

JANET LORIMER

SADDLEBACK
EDUCATIONAL PUBLISHING

QREADS

SERIES 1

- Black Widow Beauty
- Danger on Ice
- Empty Eyes
- The Experiment
- The Kula'i Street Knights
- The Mystery Quilt
- No Way to Run
- The Ritual
- The 75-Cent Son
- The Very Bad Dream

SERIES 2

- The Accuser
- Ben Cody's Treasure
- Blackout
- The Eye of the Hurricane
- The House on the Hill
- Look to the Light
- Ring of Fear
- The Tiger Lily Code
- Tug-of-War
- The White Room

SERIES 3

- The Bad Luck Play
- Breaking Point
- **Death Grip**
- Fat Boy
- No Exit
- No Place Like Home
- The Plot
- Something Dreadful Down Below
- Sounds of Terror
- The Woman Who Loved a Ghost

SERIES 4

- The Barge Ghost
- Beasts
- Blood and Basketball
- Bus 99
- The Dark Lady
- Dimes to Dollars
- Read My Lips
- Ruby's Terrible Secret
- Student Bodies
- Tough Girl

SADDLEBACK
EDUCATIONAL PUBLISHING
www.sdlback.com

ISBN-13: 978-1-61651-200-2
ISBN-10: 1-61651-200-8
eBook: 978-1-60291-922-8

Printed in Malaysia

20 19 18 17 16 4 5 6 7 8

■ ■ ■

"Will you just *look* at this awful place!" Katie wailed as she slammed on the brakes.

Bernie Polansky shook his head in disgust as he climbed out of the car. What was *with* this girl? Katie O'Neal was far too emotional for his taste.

She had stopped the car just a few inches short of a heavy iron gate. The sign that arched high over the gate read: *Oak Haven Hospital.*

Katie climbed out of the car and glanced around. "This place looks like the end of the world!" She shivered. "It's hard to believe it used to be a hospital. Seems more like a prison!"

Bernie didn't say so, but he had to agree. A dense forest bordered each side of the road. A high fence topped with barbed wire extended deep into the woods. Anyone trying to leave the hospital grounds without permission would have had a *very* hard time.

"Do you have the key?" Bernie asked. When Katie looked up, he pointed to the heavy chain and padlock on the gate.

Katie fished a key from her jeans pocket and handed it to Bernie. "Why would anyone want to keep the gate locked?" she wondered aloud. "My supervisor said this old hospital has been empty for more than 50 years."

Bernie didn't answer. The lock was a little rusty, and the key stuck. He jiggled it gently.

"Need help?" Katie asked as she crowded in next to him and reached out for the key.

Bernie glanced at her impatiently. "You may not believe this," he said, "but I can actually unlock a padlock! I'm not as helpless as you seem to think."

Katie's cheeks turned red. "I didn't mean—" she started to say.

Bernie turned away and went back to work. Just a few seconds later, the rusty padlock snapped open.

Katie got in the car and drove through the iron gate. She glanced at her watch as she waited for Bernie to close the gate and join her. When he climbed in, she impatiently gunned the engine and the car jerked forward.

Bernie glanced sideways at his work partner. Her bad mood was written all over her face. He gritted his teeth. This was *not* going to be a fun day!

Katie and Bernie worked for a maintenance company. The company did all kinds of jobs—from cleaning office buildings to making minor repairs. Bernie had only been hired two weeks ago. This was the first time he and Katie had been paired up. Right now, he was hoping it would be the last!

■ ■ ■

Katie knew that Bernie had epilepsy—a condition that can cause brief disturbances in the brain's electrical functions. The trouble was, she didn't know much about the disorder. Bernie could tell she was scared of him.

Their supervisor had explained to Katie that Bernie would be fine. He controlled his condition with medication. But Katie was nervous. She was afraid that Bernie would have a seizure while they were working together.

Bernie had run into people like Katie all his life. Once they found out he had epilepsy, they treated him differently. He was tired of having to prove himself.

"Oh, wow! Look at that!" Katie said as she drove out of the woods. Just ahead lay acres of rolling green lawns studded with large oaks and pines.

The road wound in front of a huge, three-story white building. "Oak Haven

Hospital," Katie said. "You know, until yesterday, I'd never heard of this place."

"You're kidding!" Bernie gazed at her in amazement. "Oak Haven played a big part in the history of the city. This hospital is over 100 years old."

Katie glanced at Bernie in surprise. "How do you know?"

Bernie grinned. "I love history," he told her. He studied the stately white building. "There are a lot of interesting stories about this place," he went on. "This hospital was one of the few that took in patients with highly contagious diseases like cholera and typhoid. That was long before modern medicine."

"Maybe that's why the fence is so high," Katie said, shifting the car to a lower gear. "They wanted to make sure the patients stayed inside."

She drove slowly by the hospital. "The city plans to turn this place into a park and museum," Katie went on. "City workers have already cleaned out the hospital. They're going to start restoring it soon. We're here to clean out a little cottage. It's supposed to be somewhere on the grounds behind the hospital."

Bernie frowned. "Why didn't the city people clean out the cottage, too?"

Katie shrugged. "Who knows? But the pay is good, so don't complain."

Without knowing why, Bernie got the feeling that there was something *wrong* with the cottage.

■ ■ ■

They pulled up in front of the cottage. "This little place looks like something out of a Disney movie," Bernie said. Then Katie parked the car, and they began to unload their cleaning equipment.

"Why do you say that?" she asked, handing Bernie a broom.

"Look at it," Bernie said. "What a great setting."

Katie stopped what she was doing and studied the cottage. It needed fresh paint, but there was something very charming about the place. A neat stone path wound its way to the front door. The yard was shaded by a big oak tree, and the front windows were decorated with flower boxes.

"It's picture perfect. There's even a white picket fence," Bernie said.

But inside the cottage, the feeling was very different. Perhaps it was because the oak tree cut off sunlight. Or it could have been the dismal shade of gray paint on the walls. Maybe it was just the dead air inside.

Almost at once Katie felt a chill. "It must be 20 degrees colder in here than it is outside," she said.

Bernie raised a questioning eyebrow. "Huh? I'm not a bit cold. Are you sure you're feeling okay?"

Katie glared at him. "Do you suppose we could get some heat in here?" She pointed to the small fireplace.

Bernie put down his load of cleaning supplies and lit the log that was there. Katie shivered as she moved closer to it.

"I'm going to take a look at the rest of

the cottage," Bernie said, starting down the tiny hall.

"I'm right behind you," Katie said. Bernie glanced over his shoulder at her. Was it his imagination, or did her voice sound anxious?

"I wonder who lived here," Bernie said as they peered into the small bedroom at the back.

"Maybe a gardener," Katie said.

Bernie pointed at the frilly lace curtains and the single cot.

"Maybe a nurse." Katie shrugged and blew on her hands.

Bernie opened the closet and let out a low whistle. "Look at this, O'Neal!" He pulled out a dust-covered dress. It looked like a costume from a very old black-and-white movie. "Wow! This little number must be over 70 years old!"

He shook his head in amazement. "And get a load of the furniture! Have you noticed how *old* it is? These pieces may not look like much, but I'd swear that half of them are genuine antiques."

He turned around to see if Katie was

listening. She had a funny look on her face. "What's wrong?" he asked.

"Haven't you noticed the odor?" Katie asked. "It smells *awful* in here."

Bernie sniffed, then shook his head. "The air is stuffy, that's all," he said. "I'll open a window."

"No!" Katie snapped. "I'm already too cold." She rubbed her arms. "Aren't there any other fireplaces in here?"

"You'll warm up soon enough when you get down to work," Bernie told her. "Where do we start?"

"The parlor. Where else?" Katie said.

Bernie stared at her in surprise. "You're joking. The *what?*"

"I said let's start in the front room." Irritated, Katie had raised her voice as if she were talking to a deaf person.

"No, you didn't," Bernie said. "You called it the *parlor.*"

Katie frowned at him. "I did not! You're nuts. Or maybe you're hearing things. Is that because you have—"

She bit back the rest of her sentence. Bernie could feel anger welling up inside him. *"Epilepsy?"* he asked coldly. "No, it's not. At least I don't feel cold when it's warm, and my sense of smell isn't all messed up."

Katie turned abruptly and stalked back to the front room. "You start on that end of the room, and I'll start here," she told Bernie. "If you find any papers, put them in a box. The boss said to save any old papers we find. We need to move the furniture outside, too."

Bernie opened the old rolltop desk. Inside he found a stack of newspaper clippings dating back to 1910. The ink had faded, and the paper had yellowed and become brittle with age. But Bernie could still read the print.

"Hey, Polansky, get busy!"

Bernie glanced up and saw Katie watching him. "You said to put papers—"

"I didn't say you had to *read* each one," Katie snapped. "Just put them all in the box. I'd like to get out of here." She glanced around nervously.

Bernie frowned. "What's bothering you, O'Neal?"

"Nothing," she said. Then, dropping her voice, she added, "I just get the weirdest feeling that—that—"

"That what?" Bernie prompted. He sensed that her fear was real.

"I don't know," she said. "I feel like someone is watching us. Someone—" She glanced around. "—or *something!*"

■ ■ ■

Bernie kept on boxing papers, but his thoughts weren't entirely on his work. Katie's words echoed in his mind.

Something? She was trying to hide it, but he could tell she was scared. And why was she so cold? She'd borrowed his jacket to put on over hers. Something—but what?—was very wrong with Katie O'Neal.

"Great, just great," Bernie thought in disgust. "Here I am, stuck in the middle of nowhere with a bossy woman who's also losing her mind."

"Oh, I don't know why I bother!" Katie threw her cleaning rag down in disgust. She dropped into a chair. "It's all so hopeless!" She started to cry.

Bernie stared at her in surprise. "What's hopeless, O'Neal?"

"All of it—everything." Her lower lip trembled. "But who's to believe a poor Irish girl?"

Slivers of ice slid down Bernie's spine. He had guessed Katie was Irish because of her name and flaming red hair. But she didn't strike him as the type of person who felt sorry for herself. Maybe she'd just been working too hard.

"Let's take a break," he said quickly. "Tell you what—let's go outside where it's warmer."

He didn't wait for an answer. He grabbed his Thermos of hot coffee and dragged Katie out the door.

■ ■ ■

The change in Katie was amazing. Sitting on the lawn in the sunshine, she was her old self again. "How much progress are you making on your end of the room?" she asked.

"I'm doing okay," he answered. "One thing seems strange, though. I haven't found any letters or a journal. Nothing the person who lived here wrote. Nothing to identify who lived in the cottage."

Katie looked puzzled. "So?"

Bernie didn't know how to explain why that seemed so odd. Instead, he changed the subject. "How are you doing with *your* end of the room?"

Katie shrugged. "Okay. It's just a dumb cleaning job. Pretty dull!"

Bernie studied her for a moment. "Not—*hopeless?"* he asked.

Katie gave him a funny look. "Hopeless? That's a weird thing to say. What's wrong with you, Polansky? What can be hopeless about getting rid of dust and cobwebs?"

"Nothing." Didn't she remember her own words? "Do you think we'll finish the job today?" he asked.

"Sure—if we keep at it," Katie said,

scrambling to her feet. "Come on, let's get back to work."

Bernie was a little worried. What in the world could account for Katie's strange behavior?

Back in the cottage, Bernie watched Katie closely for a few minutes. She seemed to be all right, so he went back to work clearing out the desk.

In the last drawer, he found a framed photo. He rubbed dust off the glass. It was a faded black-and-white picture of a young woman with large dark eyes. She was dressed in the style of the early 1900s. The photographer had posed her holding a pretty little straw hat decorated with roses made of ribbons.

Suddenly, Bernie felt Katie standing at his elbow. "What did you find?" she asked.

"Oh, it's just a picture," he said, holding it up.

Katie gasped. "Oh, how grand she looked that day!"

Bernie stared at Katie in disbelief. "What

are you talking about?" he asked.

"She was dressed in her best," Katie went on, her blue eyes sparkling as she talked. "She wore that pretty little hat. But the photographer told her to take it off. He wanted her to show off her beautiful hair."

Katie laughed, but the sound was unnatural. It chilled Bernie to the bone.

"Her hair was her crowning glory," Katie went on. "It was so long she could sit on it! And black and shiny as a raven's wing. Truly a sight to see."

The frame slipped from Bernie's hand and fell to the floor. When the glass shattered, he barely noticed.

"Oh, now look what you've done!" Katie scolded.

She leaned over to pick up the broken glass, but Bernie pulled her upright. "Katie, you sound like you know who this girl is," he said.

■ ■ ■

"Well, of course I do," Katie said. "Molly Murphy was her name. Born in County Kerry, Ireland in 1875. She came to these United States in 1891."

Bernie took a deep breath. He was horribly aware that Katie was now speaking with a broad Irish accent.

"She wanted to send a picture of herself to her family in Ireland," Katie went on. Then her smile disappeared. "Only by then, it was too late for her."

"What do you mean, 'too late'?" Bernie demanded. But Katie only shook her head. Her lips trembled and her eyes filled with tears.

"You told me you knew nothing about this place," Bernie said. He reached down and pulled the photo loose from the broken frame. He waved it in Katie's face. "So how do you know her name and when she was born?"

Katie's eyes blazed with anger. "I *know,* all right!" she cried out. "I'll even show you where she rests her head, poor tortured soul!" With that, Katie plunged across the room and out the door.

Bernie ran after her. "Katie, *wait!*" he yelled. What was happening?

At the top of a low rise, she stopped outside a fenced enclosure. As he drew closer, Bernie saw that it was a small graveyard. For a moment, he wondered who could be buried there. Perhaps these were the graves of patients who had died alone and in poverty.

"There!" Katie pointed through the bars of the fence at a small granite headstone. "See?"

Bernie looked at the lettering carved into the stone. *"Molly Murphy,"* he read aloud. *"Born, 1875. Died, 1942."*

He looked up at Katie. Something alien—something *not* Katie—looked back at him through her blue eyes.

"Who are you?" Bernie whispered.

Her laughter chilled him. "Molly Murphy, if you please."

■ ■ ■

Bernie was stunned. He didn't know what to think or say. While he hesitated, Katie spun about on her heel and headed back to the cottage.

Bernie hurried after her. "Katie!" he called out. "Wait!"

He grabbed her shoulder to stop her. As she turned, Katie's face twisted with anger. "Take your filthy hands off me, John Moffit!" she yelled. Then, her eyes narrowing, she studied his face. "But *you're* not John Moffit!"

"No, I—" Bernie started to say, but she cut him off with a shake of her head.

"You may not be John Moffit, but you're no better!" she exclaimed. "You're all villains from the Board of Health."

Bernie thought that Katie must have lost her mind.

He glanced around. As far as he could tell, the grounds of the old hospital were deserted. He wondered how he could get her out of here. And where Katie had put the car keys?

Katie turned away and continued down the hill. Bernie followed. Now he remembered seeing her shove the car keys into her jeans pocket. Then he remembered the cell phone. Had Katie brought it into the cottage? Or was it still in the car?

"So you thought you'd get the best of me." Katie tossed the words over her shoulder. "Because I'm only a poor Irish girl who can neither read nor write?"

Her words startled Bernie. "That's why I couldn't find any letters or a journal," he thought to himself. "Molly Murphy was illiterate!"

He drew his breath in sharply. Was it possible that the restless spirit of Molly Murphy had actually taken over the body of Katie O'Neal?

■ ■ ■

"I don't believe in ghosts," Bernie thought to himself. "Or do I?"

All of a sudden it didn't matter what he believed. Either Katie thought she was Molly, or Molly really had taken over Katie's mind and body.

Now Bernie could guess why the city workers hadn't cleaned out the cottage. Maybe they'd felt uncomfortable in the little house. Or perhaps Molly's ghost had come forward and tried to work her mischief on them, too.

"I've got to find out why Molly was so angry," Bernie thought. "Until I know that, there's no way I can help her."

Back in the cottage, Katie headed directly for the bedroom.

"I'll show you my pretty hat," she said. She pulled an old hatbox from the closet shelf, opened it, and lifted out a small straw hat. The brim was decorated with faded pink ribbon roses.

Bernie tried to stay calm. How could Katie have known the color of the roses? She *couldn't*—unless she'd been taken over by Molly's ghost!

As she softly hummed a tune, Katie tried on the hat. "There now," she said in her lilting Irish accent. "What do you think of that?"

"Very nice indeed," Bernie said. "So tell me, Molly, why are you so angry at John Moffit?"

Her smile soured. "Because he's the one who put me here—villain that he is! Wasn't it John Moffit who made everyone believe all those terrible lies about me?"

Bernie was getting into it. In a strange way, this conversation was getting more and more interesting. "What lies?" he asked.

"That I'm a murderer!" she wailed as she tossed the hat aside and sat down on the narrow cot. She put her hands over her face and sobbed. *"Me!* Molly Murphy, who never hurt a fly. They said I killed the children. Oh, cruel lies!"

Bernie frowned, trying to figure out what else to ask her. Suddenly, her hands dropped and Katie looked into his eyes. "Bernie?" she said weakly.

■ ■ ■

Bernie gasped. "Katie?" He dropped to the floor next to her, seizing her hands in his. "Katie, is that you?"

"Bernie, help—" She took a deep breath. Then Bernie could actually see her change again! Her blue eyes began to darken and the corners of her mouth turned down unhappily.

"How often do I have to say my name before you'll believe me?" Her voice rose sharply. "You want the world to forget all about the little Irish girl that you've imprisoned." Molly was back!

Bernie's mind was racing. "Molly's got a death grip on Katie from beyond the grave," he thought. "But for just a moment, I saw Katie! So there's hope!"

He hurried back to the front room and carefully lifted the old newspaper clippings from the box.

"The answer must be in here," Bernie thought as he began to read. Within 10 minutes he discovered why Molly was so angry.

But getting rid of her would not be easy.

Suddenly he realized how quiet the cottage was. He hurried down the hall. Katie had fallen asleep on the cot.

"Or is it Molly who's all worn out?" Bernie wondered.

"Come on, wake up!" Bernie called out. He shook Katie's shoulder. She opened her blue eyes and gazed at him in bewilderment. Then, in the next instant, her eyes darkened and he saw Molly glaring at him!

"Molly, you say you don't like hurting people," Bernie said.

"Why, of course not!" she snapped as she struggled to sit up.

"Are you *sure?*" Bernie yanked Katie to her feet. She gave a yelp of surprise as he pushed her across the room to the mirror. "Look!" he exclaimed.

She gazed at her reflection, a small frown drawing her brows together.

"That's not Molly Murphy," Bernie said. "That's Katie O'Neal! Look at her! Look at her red hair."

The dark eyes widened.

"You've stolen Katie's body, and that's hurting her!" Bernie went on.

The dark eyes filled with tears. "But I *need* her!" Molly exclaimed in a pitiful wail. "I've been waiting so long to tell the world about the wrong that was done to me. I need—"

"It's time to let go," Bernie cut in. "Look, Molly! This is your chance to make up for the suffering you caused those parents so long ago."

"It wasn't my fault!" she wailed, the tears spilling down her cheeks. "I never wanted those dear children to get sick."

"I know," Bernie said gently. "But that's all in the past, Molly. Katie lives in the present. She deserves to live her own life. If you let Katie go, I'll make sure no one forgets what happened to you. And I'll do my best to see that it never happens again."

Molly threw her head back and gave out an awful cry of despair. Then Katie slumped into Bernie's arms.

■ ■ ■

"Who was Molly Murphy, and what was the price she paid?" Katie asked. She bit into her sandwich as she waited for Bernie's answer.

Bernie took a sip of coffee. They were sitting on the lawn outside the cottage, taking their lunch break. Bernie had a hard time believing that just half an hour ago he'd fought with a ghost.

Katie shuddered. "It was so weird. I could see and hear—but someone else was doing the talking and thinking."

"Molly Murphy," Bernie said. "She was a young Irish woman who came to America in the late 1800s. Like other immigrants, she wanted a better life. But Molly couldn't read or write. That made it hard for her to find well-paid work. Finally she was hired as a nanny. Unfortunately, the children she was caring for got sick with typhoid fever. They all died."

Katie shook her head sadly.

"Then a doctor named John Moffit discovered that Molly was a carrier of typhoid fever," Bernie went on. "That's why the Board of Health isolated her in the cottage. She was never allowed to leave. She finally died here!"

Katie frowned. "What's a 'carrier'?"

"Carriers are people who have a deadly bacteria in their bodies. They don't get sick themselves, but they can infect others," Bernie said. "Mary Mallon was another typhoid carrier. She's famous! Haven't you ever heard the name 'Typhoid Mary'?"

Katie shook her head.

"Mary Mallon caused a number of deaths. Other carriers caused even more, but Mary was punished more than any other carrier."

"Why?" Katie asked.

"She had a lot going against her," Bernie answered. "For one thing, she was poor. Strike one! She was also illiterate. Strike two! And she was a woman. Strike three!"

Katie's eyes opened wide. "But that's discrimination!"

Bernie grinned. "There's more. Typhoid

Mary and Molly Murphy were both Irish. That's strike four! A hundred years ago, the Irish suffered terrible prejudice in America. Many people thought the Irish were stupid and lazy—so they were very badly treated."

Katie's eyes widened in anger. "That's ridiculous," she exclaimed. "I'm Irish. And I'm not stupid or lazy!"

Bernie nodded. "Just as you said, that's discrimination. Prejudice because of race, national origin, age, or gender is still very common."

His voice trailed away, but his glance was fixed on Katie's face. "There are other types of prejudice," he added. "Take me, for example. When some people find out that I have epilepsy, they jump to all kinds of ignorant conclusions."

■ ■ ■

Katie's cheeks turned bright red. "Oh, Bernie—" She stopped. "I—I'm sorry. I—I guess I did, too."

"You haven't exactly made an effort to find

out what my strengths and weaknesses are," Bernie told her. "Or even what epilepsy is all about. Think about this, for example. Did you know that more than 50 million people around the world have epilepsy? With medication, almost all of them lead normal lives."

Katie's eyes widened. "I didn't know. I—" She shrugged and smiled. "Okay, Bernie, why don't you educate me?"

Bernie grinned. "That could take a lot of time, O'Neal. Are we going to be working together after today?"

"Are you kidding?" She gazed at him in surprise. "You saved my life. That means I owe you! Besides, we haven't finished cleaning out the cottage. And I don't plan to go back in there alone!"

Bernie burst out laughing. "Agreed."

"So how do you plan to keep your promise to Molly? Are you really going to tell her story?" Katie asked.

Bernie thought for a moment. Then he smiled. "You said the city plans to turn the hospital into a museum. Wouldn't a Molly

Murphy display be perfect for it?"

"You bet!" Katie said excitedly. "You've already got a good start. There are the news clippings, the photo—"

"Molly's display wouldn't be only about the past," Bernie said. "It would also be about the present. About what fear and ignorance still do to people—and the way we all deserve to be treated."

A breeze touched Bernie's cheek. But *was* it a breeze? Or was it a soft, ghostly hand saying goodbye?

After-Reading Wrap-Up

1. What was unusual about Oak Haven Hospital?

2. Molly would leave Katie alone only if she was able to take care of some unfinished business. What was it?

3. What did Molly and Bernie have in common?

4. In your opinion, what was the most interesting part of the book? Describe the part in detail.

5. How did Katie change when she became Molly?

6. What if Bernie hadn't convinced Molly to leave Katie alone? Predict what might have happened in a future scene.